FEATHERS LIKE A RAINBOW

An Amazon Indian Tale

Story and Pictures by Flora

Harper & Row, Publishers

Acknowledgments

With special thanks to Scott A. Mori; Ghillean Tolmie Prance, director of the Royal Botanic Gardens at Kew in London and the author of *Algumas Flores da Amazonia*, a book that proved invaluable to me in my research of the flowers of the Amazon; and João Barbosa Rodrigues, my great-grandfather and the author of *Poranduba Amazonense*, a story of the Amazon Indians—it was from this book that I learned the legend of the hummingbird.

Library of Congress Cataloging-in-Publication Data
Flora.
   Feathers like a rainbow / by Flora. — 1st ed.
     p.   cm.
   Summary: The birds in the forests surrounding the Amazon River all have dark feathers until they decide to steal some colors from the Hummingbird.
    ISBN 0-06-021837-1 : $. — ISBN 0-06-021838-X (lib. bdg.) : $
   [1. Birds—Fiction. 2. Amazon River Valley—Fiction.] I. Title.
PZ7.F6625Fe 1989   88-26788
[E]—dc19   CIP
                               AC

To my husband, Henry Potter Lage

A long, long time ago, the birds of the great rain forest around the Amazon River had dark feathers.

"Why are our feathers so ugly?" Jacamin, a gray-winged trumpeter, asked his mother. "Why can't I have feathers as beautiful as the rainbow? Why can't I have feathers as bright as the flowers and butter-flies we see around us?"

"I will try to find the colors for you, my son," his mother promised.

As Jacamin's mother walked through the forest, she met Macaw.

"Hello, my friend," she said. "Do you know where I can find colors as beautiful as the rainbow and as bright as the flowers and butterflies of the rain forest? I want them for my son's feathers."

"No," replied Macaw, "but I too would like some color in my feathers. Let us search together."

As the two birds walked deeper and deeper into the forest, they met many other birds. They all wanted bright colors for their feathers.

But they looked in vain.

By the end of the day, the birds were tired and discouraged. "We'll never find the colors," said Macaw.

Suddenly something bright and brilliant darted by.

"What was that?" cried Toucan.

"It can't be a firefly, fireflies only shine in the dark of the night," said Macaw.

"It flew too quickly to be a butterfly," said Ibis.

"It was too close to be a star," said Woodpecker.

"Look! It is a tiny bird!" cried Cock-of-the-rock.

The tiny bird was covered with feathers so bright the birds had to blink their eyes. They watched it hover in the air and flit from flower to flower.

"What is your name, and where did you get your beautiful feathers?" Jacamin's mother asked.

"I am Hummingbird, and I get my beautiful feathers from the flowers," said the bird. "Every day I kiss the flowers of the rain forest. From each I take a dab of color and drop it into my bowl. Then I splash a little of each color on my feathers."

The other birds could hardly wait for the next day. They all wanted to copy Hummingbird! As soon as the sun rose, they rushed to the flowers. But most of the birds were too heavy to hover in the air, and their beaks were too big to reach inside the flowers the way Hummingbird's did. "It's useless," said Macaw sadly.

Jacamin's mother was saddest of all. She had promised to find the colors for her son. Then, suddenly, she had an idea. She would steal the bowl of colors from Hummingbird!

She grabbed the bowl and hurried home.

"Here, my son," she said. "I have brought you Hummingbird's colors. Go quickly and wash yourself in the bowl before the other birds see you."

But it was too late!
The birds swooped down on
Jacamin and snatched away the
bowl. Then they bathed themselves
in Hummingbird's colors. Macaw
took red, orange, green, and blue.
Woodpecker took red and blue.
Toucan took green, yellow, and red,
and Ibis pink. Cock-of-the-rock
took bright orange.

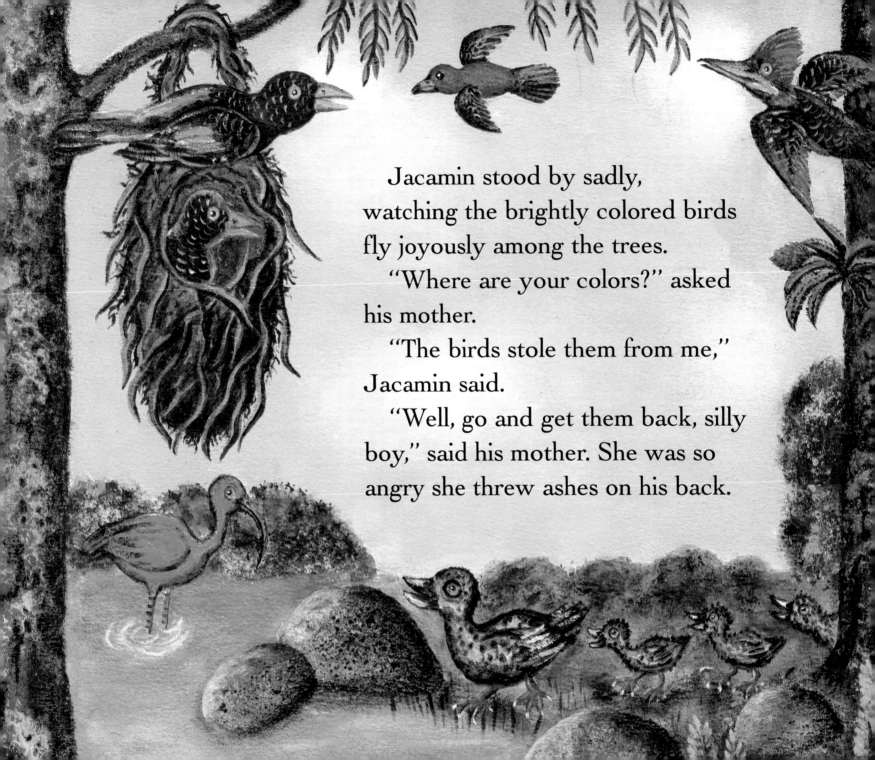

Jacamin stood by sadly,
watching the brightly colored birds
fly joyously among the trees.

"Where are your colors?" asked
his mother.

"The birds stole them from me,"
Jacamin said.

"Well, go and get them back, silly
boy," said his mother. She was so
angry she threw ashes on his back.

When Jacamin got to Hummingbird's bowl, there was only a dot of purple left. He rubbed it on his breast.

To this very day the gray-winged trumpeter has a purple breast and an ash-gray back.

As for the other birds of the Amazon, they too still wear the colors stolen from Hummingbird so long ago.

Only the hummingbird has *all* the colors. His feathers are as beautiful as the rainbow, and as bright as the flowers and butterflies of the great rain forest around the Amazon River.